While You Were Out . . .

The Adventures of

Tulip & Piggy

in Magical Merida

ISBN: 0999522116

ISBN-13: 978-0999522110 (Katy Warren)

While You Were Out . . .

The Adventures of

Tulip & Piggy

in Magical Merida

By Katy Warren

(and Tulip & Piggy)

For Eliza, Xander,
Esther, & Iris

While You Were Out . . .

The Adventures of

Tulip & Piggy

in Magical Merida

By Katy Warren

Dear Reader,

Have you ever wondered what *your* stuffed animals get up to when you're not at home? Turn the page to find out what kind of fun we had in Mexico while Eliza was out!

Love, Tulip and Piggy

Magical Merida

Two weeks in **Merida, Mexico!** A very exciting trip for a bunny and a pig who were used to living in Seattle with their best friend, Eliza.

But that wasn't all. On the first night in Merida, Tulip and Piggy discovered the most AMAZING thing. They were able to WRITE to Eliza! For the first time ever! Usually Eliza would talk to the animals, but she couldn't hear them when they talked back. Very frustrating indeed, for a couple of chatty friends.

When Eliza left the casa on the first day, Tulip and Piggy were a bit freaked out by being in a brand new place, but she came back from her day in Merida with gifts!

Dear Eliza,

Thank you for giving me this great hammock! I was really comfortable last night, even though Piggy was snoring and woke me up three times.

Love, Tulip

Dear Eliza,

Don't believe everything Tulip says. I do **NOT** snore. I am a quiet and polite pig at all times. Oh, and thank you very much for letting me sleep in the new hammock. It was very comfy.

Love, Piggy.

A Day at the Pool

Tulip and Piggy soon learned that there were many fun new things that they could do while Eliza was out. Every day Eliza and the rest of the people would leave the casa, and Tulip and Piggy would plan their day.

Day 1 Plan: Swimming!

Piggy even found a rope just in case he had to lasso Tulip out of the pool in an emergency. Hmmm, maybe Piggy needs some lifeguard lessons. That's not usually the best method for saving bunnies.

Dear Eliza,

Can you have a word with Tulip? She jumped in the pool and splashed me completely! SO RUDE!!! I think she needs an etiquette class ASAP.

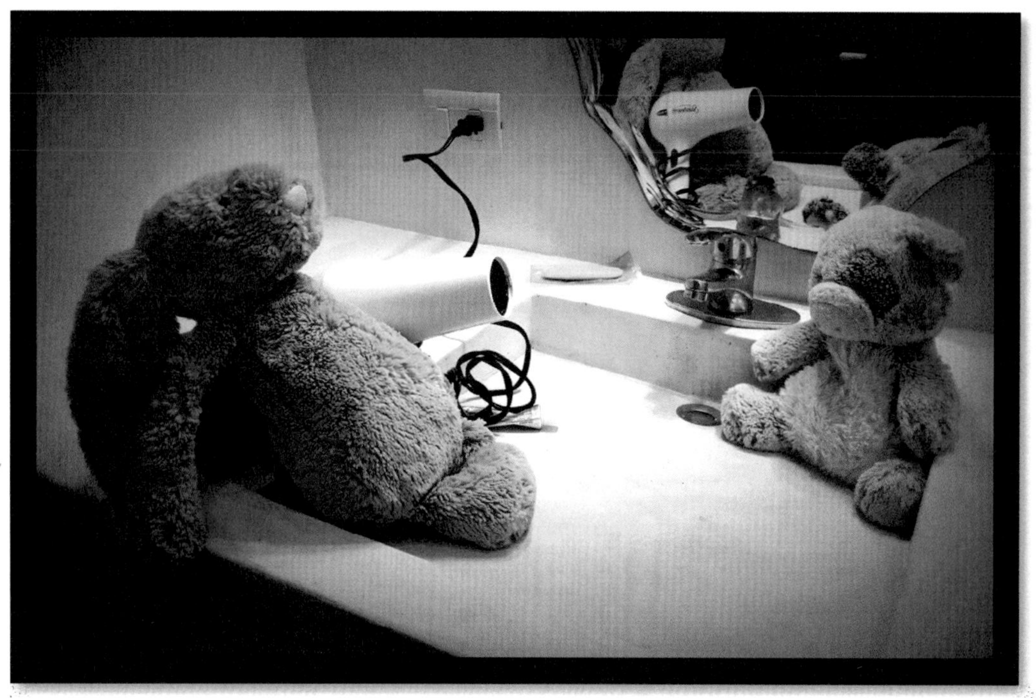

Love, Piggy

Dear Eliza,

While you were out today, Piggy & I went swimming in the pool! It was extremely fun. I had to use a noodle to float, but Piggy knows how to swim. Anyway, he gave me some good tips so I could learn.

The problem came when we got out. I was totally furry and dripping all over the place! Fortunately Piggy found a hairdryer under the bathroom sink and we blew ourselves dry.

What a day!

Love, Tulip

Road Trip

Dear Eliza,

Road Trip today! Piggy and I decided to go to Izamal, the gold city, since we heard you guys talking about it. It was challenging to get there, let me tell you, but it was a great day.

Did you know that gold is my third favorite color (after pink and turquoise)? And that that whole darn town was gold!

Piggy and I snuck onto a horse-drawn carriage with some tourists from Walla Walla, and we got quite a tour. Our horse was named Poinsettia, which is a nice name and all, but not as nice as Tulip.

Love, Tulip

Dear Eliza,

Did you have a fun day? We did! I'm sure Tulip told you about Izamal, but did she tell you how we got there?

The cabs would not stop for a bunny and a pig, so Tulip grabbed my hoof and used her giant bunny feet to LEAP up on a truck driving by. We jumped off at the bus station, and then snuck into a lady's bag to get on the bus since we didn't have tickets.

Do I smell like tortillas a little bit? Because that lady had a lot of tortillas in her bag.

Love, Piggy

The Dog Next Door

Dear Eliza,

Today was a bit annoying, but I think I have things sorted out now. Piggy and I were hanging out in the big hammock (yesterday was a tough day!) when we were rudely interrupted by that silly dog next door barking his fool head off.

Well! I was not going to tolerate that. I marched out to the pool, leaped to the top of the wall, and gave that dog (his name is Pepe) a stern talking-to. I really showed him who's boss, I'll tell you. We won't have any problem with Pepe from here on out.

Love Tulip

Dear Eliza,

That dimwit dog next door was a major pain in my fluffy pink behind today. And Tulip, who totally thinks she's in charge of the world, flew out to the back wall to give Pepe a snooty lecture, like you know she likes to do.

The thing is, Tulip is positive that Pepe is going to follow all those rules she was yelling about, but I scampered up that palm tree and I could see Pepe just drooling and scratching his ears during the lecture. So I'm afraid Tulip is going to be very disappointed and annoyed when he starts up again!

Love, Piggy

Iris Comes Home

Dear Eliza,

It's so exciting that you brought home Iris! She is our first Mexican friend, if you don't count Poinsettia the horse.

Iris said she saw you in front of the giant Pyramid and KNEW that you were destined to meet. She concentrated *very* hard and says that she thinks her mind messages convinced you to come to her table.
I don't know about that crazy notion, but I like her anyway.

Love, Tulip

Dear Eliza,

Are you aware that Iris is from some-place called Chicken Pizza? That seems a bit strange, but hey, I don't know much about Mexico yet. I'll go ask Iris.

Love, Piggy

Querida Eliza,

Gracias for bringing me to your casa! I wished so hard that you would come and find me, and IT WORKED!!

When I got here I was nerviosa at first, but Tulip and Piggy have been very welcoming and you are very nice too.

It is much calmer here compared to Chichen Itza where I lived before. Thousands of tourists were looking at me every day, but **you** decided to take me home. Muchisimas Gracias!

And you even have hammocks. That is exactly what I sleep in when it is caliente!

Love, Iris

p.s. Did you know that Piggy snores?

Midnight Snack

Dear Eliza,

It was hotter than a tamale last night!

We couldn't sleep and Piggy and Iris were feeling a bit peckish, so I generously made us all a snack. It was a nice way to welcome Iris. She's cheerful, but she's a little overwhelmed since she used to live outside among the pyramids and now she's in a house. Imagine how much she'll like Seattle!

She loved our midnight snack. Oh hey, sorry about the mess. After our big meal we were so exhausted we went to bed right away.

Love, Tulip

Dear Eliza,

I hope you don't mind that we moved the hammocks outside last night. Holy macaroni, was it hot! We couldn't sleep so we had a midnight snack.

Tulip took charge and prepared all rabbit food, which I like but poor Iris really wanted some meat. When we looked in the fridge she wanted to eat the leftover bacon. BACON!?!?!? I ask you!! That could be a distant relative of mine! Honestly, it's only good manners to avoid the pork products when you're with a pig friend. Iris was quite sorry and we made up and she ate the old hamburger even though we couldn't figure out the microwave.

Love, Piggy

Playing UNO

Dear Eliza,

We watched you play UNO and tried it out today.

I suspect Iris might be cheating. Otherwise I would be winning, right? I don't know. I'm going to keep trying and thinking about my strategy and maybe I'll improve and win a few times at least.

I think we may go out later, but my tummy kind of hurts after our midnight snack. I drank water out of the tap, and that may have been a bad idea. Hope I don't puke all over Iris and get her pretty dress all disgusting.

Love, Tulip

Querida Eliza,

Do you see my big smile? That is because I'm a great UNO player! I never knew I could do this. It is the first card game that I have ever played. Maybe I will go to Las Vegas and try my luck playing UNO at the casino!

Though Tulip tells me that people sometimes lose all their money doing that, so maybe I will just go home with you.

Love, Iris

Dear Eliza,

I don't think I'm going to play this game anymore. We just taught Iris how to play and she's already at UNO. Maybe she has an advantage because she speaks Spanish.

I, on the other hand, have approximately 37 stupid UNO cards. Tulip says I'm just being a bad sport.

Hmmph!! I'm gonna go do something more fun, like ride an iguana.

Love, Piggy

Around the Casa

Dear Eliza,

With all the excitement of Iris's arrival, we decided to have a quiet day at home.

Once we figured out the iPad, Piggy and I argued a bit about what to watch and eventually compromised on Bugs Bunny and Porky Pig. Of course, Bugs was the star of the show, as it should be. Bunnies are extremely good actors.

Love, Tulip

Dear Eliza,

After a few minutes of watching that mean Bugs Bunny make a fool of Porky Pig, who was only trying to do his best like any good pig, I left to find Iris.

We decided to do a Mad Lib. Can you think of a good plural noun? We're trying to decide between "rutabagas" and "furballs".

Love, Piggy

Querida Eliza,

I hear you have a cousin named Iris! I would love to meet her sometime, and also the rest of your cousins and aunts and uncles. Maybe Tulip can read us all a book about Mexico. Or if she is too shy, maybe YOU can read us a book!

Love, Iris

Neighborhood Exploring

Dear Eliza,

Piggy and Iris and I decided to explore our Merida neighborhood today.

First we got ourselves a snack at the cart at the corner. Manuel, who owns the cart, even let us do a bit of candy selling ourselves! I advised this little girl to brush her teeth when she got home. Dental health is very important.

After some shopping, we took a ride on a truck, but Iris wasn't quick enough and the truck took off without her! I feel kind of sorry for people with tiny feet. Everyone should be able to leap like bunnies, in my opinion.

Love, Tulip

Dear Eliza,

Iris was concerned that you didn't have a bag that would fit all three of us on the way back to Seattle, so we did a little bit of shopping for you. Unfortunately, you forgot to leave us any pesos, so we couldn't get you a gift like we wanted to.

Tulip is up to her old tricks giving advice to everyone whether they want it or not. Can't she just let that little girl enjoy her candy without giving her a tooth-brushing lecture? I love Tulip, but she should lighten up sometimes.

Love, Piggy

Back to Seattle

Dear Eliza,

It's sad to say adios to magical Merida, but I'm excited to get back to Seattle and our real life.

Tulip and Iris keep complaining about my snoring so I'm considering visiting a doctor when I get back. Maybe I have sleep apnea! I'd have to get one of those machines, and that would be even louder than the snoring. Ha! It would serve those two right for being too sensitive and complaining about a gentle little nighttime snort!

Love,
Piggy

Querida Eliza,

I am SO excited about going to Seattle! It will be my very first plane ride, and my first visit to the United States. I have never even been out of Yucatan State!

I am un poquito nerviosa but Tulip and Piggy say they will take care of me on the plane and introduce me to all the animals and dolls at your house. Do any of them speak Spanish and Mayan like me? That would be muy bueno, but if there are not, maybe I will start a class and they can all learn Español. I have always wanted to be a teacher.

Love, Iris

Dear Eliza,

It's been so wonderful to be able to communicate with you in this magical place! Piggy, Iris and I got together last night near the pool and sang "For She's a Jolly Good Fellow" at the top of our voices, and we did it because you ARE a jolly good fellow (or a jolly good girl, anyway). We also did it to drown out Pepe's barking for the last time.

I will miss writing to you, but remember we love you and will be thinking about you even if we can't speak out loud!

Love, Tulip

The End

Takis

We can be reached by email

tulipandpiggy@gmail.com

Made in the USA
Lexington, KY
08 December 2017